A Very Good Lie

by Cheyenne Cisco
illustrated by Maurie Manning

Table of Contents

Chapter 1
Plunk!

My name is Nikki Riggs and I tell lies.
That's what this story is about.

I was with Grams in her room
last Thursday after school.
Grams lives with us.
That day, she was pulling hats
out of her closet.
Grams was going fishing
with her buddies for two days.
A car horn beeped outside.
Her friends were waiting.

Grams pulled on a big, floppy pink hat and picked up her boots and fishing rod.

"How do I look?" she asked.

She spun around.

The rod whipped around too, and I ducked.

"You look like you are going to a tea party with fish," I said.

Grams grinned.

"Perfect," she said.

The horn beeped again.

Grams stuffed an extra hat in her bag.

"I just want to sit in a boat in the sun,"
she told me.

"I won't even put a hook on my line.

I don't want to hurt any poor fish."

That's just how Grams is.

I'd miss her while she was gone.

The car horn beeped a third time.
"I'm late!" Grams screeched. "Bye-bye!"
She waved, and the rod flicked
and hit the ceiling.
Then she grabbed her bag
and bumped it down the stairs.
I heard *thump, thump, clomp, crash, slam.*
And she was gone.

I looked around the room.

Dirty socks, open magazines,

and knitting stuff were thrown all around.

Grams is messy, like me.

My sister Kendra and Mom

are the neat ones.

I picked up a scarf and a book

from the floor.

Under the scarf, something glittered.

It was a necklace.

A silver lion's head dangled from a chain.

I knew all about that necklace.
Grams and Grandpa traveled
all over the world before Grandpa died.
He got a gift for Grams in each place.
The lion necklace came from Africa.
In Kenya, a lion jumped right up
onto the windshield of their car,
and Grandpa fainted.
Grams got that necklace out sometimes
just to look at it, and she told the story
of the scary lion every time.
I ran a finger over the lines
in the lion's mane.
He was so beautiful.

I took the necklace into the bathroom
so I could hold it up to my neck
and see how it looked in the mirror.
The lion was not just pretty.
It was wild, with sharp teeth.
I loved it.
I had to put it on, just for a little while.

I knew Grams might not want me
to wear it.
But I pushed that thought away.
I reached up to clip the necklace
around my neck.
Then my fingers slipped.
The necklace and chain slid
out of my hands
and landed with a *plunk*.

Right in the toilet.

Chapter 2
Toilet Water

I looked down into the water.
The necklace was at the bottom
of the toilet bowl, way in the back.
You could just barely see it.
"This is not a problem," I thought.
"I just have to reach in there.
It's just water."

I stared down.

It looked clean enough, I guess,

but how clean can a toilet really be?

I leaned closer.

That didn't help.

It made me think about throwing up.

But I had to do this, for Grams.

She would be so upset if she lost

that necklace!

"I'm going to get it now," I said out loud.

But my hand stayed by my side.

I made up my mind to count to three.

Then I'd stick my hand in the water, fast.

And then I'd wash my hands for three hours.

Maybe I'd take a shower, too.

I started to count.

"One."

"Two."

"Three!"

But I didn't move.

I just couldn't make myself do it.

Maybe I could just forget it?

No one knew I dropped the necklace in there.

But then I thought about Grams.

She'd miss the necklace.

She'd be upset,

and it would be my fault.

I couldn't stand that.

I *had* to get the necklace out.

I grabbed the phone
and called Ronny Donaldson.
Ronny lives next door.
He knows a lot about how things work.
Ronny's not a bad guy,
but he is such a nerd.
Sometimes he gets excited and falls
off his chair in class.
I try not to be seen with him at school.
"Ronny," I said. "Quick.
Tell me how to get something
out of a toilet."

He said, "I read once about a toilet that exploded."

If you ask me, Ronny reads too much.

He said, "This lady threw paper towels in the toilet and they had. . . ."

"Ronny!" I said. "Focus!

I dropped a necklace in the toilet. I can't reach in and get it. What do I do?"

"Oh," Ronny said.

"Why don't you. . . ."

Just then I heard my mother's voice.

"Kendra? Nikki! Get down here, now!"

That didn't sound good.

I told Ronny I'd call him back.

Chapter 3
Tick, Tock, Dead Clock

Mom was waiting in the living room,
and she looked angry.

Really angry.

"Who did that?" she asked.

She pointed at the floor.

Grandpa's clock was lying there.

Part of the wood was broken off,
and you could see some of the clock guts.

They looked bent and dead.

"Well?" Mom asked.

"This clock didn't fall off the table
on its own.

Who broke it?"

Nobody said anything.

But when I looked up from the clock,
Kendra and Mom were staring at me.

"Hey!" I cried.

"Don't look at *me*!"

I didn't break the clock.

Kendra must have done it.

But Kendra said, "Come on, Nikki.

You are always doing stuff like this.

Who tried to make green slime

and broke Mom's bowl last week?

So just admit it!"

Kendra and I are twins,

but she is 25 minutes older than me.

She thinks that makes her the Big Sister.

I think it makes her a Big Pain.

"Mom!" I said. "I didn't do it!"

"Tell the truth, Nikki," Mom said.

A stab of surprise hit my chest.

She thought I was lying!

I felt so hurt I couldn't say a word.

"Grandpa made this clock
with his own hands," Mom said.
"Your grandmother will be so upset
when she sees it!"
Mom bent to pick up the clock.
She said, "I expect one of you to tell me
how this happened
before your grandmother gets back."
She said "one of you,"
but she was looking at me.

Chapter 4
The Bet

I told myself not to feel hurt,

to forget the clock.

I had a bigger problem.

That necklace.

Would it turn black from sitting in the water?

I ran back upstairs

and called Ronny again.

"Don't worry," Ronny told me.

"I'll help you get the necklace out.

But we're going to have dinner in a few minutes.

How about tomorrow after school?

No one will flush it before then, will they?"

Yipes! Flushing!

I thought about it.

"I don't think so," I told him.

"Grams is the only one who uses this bathroom,
and she went fishing."

We agreed to meet the next day after school,
and I started to hang up.

"Um, Nikki?" he said.

"What?"

"I'm going to that party
on Saturday afternoon," Ronny said.
His voice squeaked on the "I'm."
"You know, the school's 100th birthday thing.
Do you want to go with me?
There will be game booths and a band
for dancing."
Dancing?
When Ronny walks, he looks like
one of those long, skinny puppets on strings.
When he runs, he tends to fall down.

I like Ronny just fine.

But I couldn't dance with him.

Not where actual people would see!

I had to think fast.

"Sorry," I said.

"I told Kendra I'd teach her how to ride
my skateboard on Saturday.

We're going to the skate park."

It was quiet on the other end of the phone.

What was Ronny thinking?

Did he know I made up the skateboard thing?

He might.

He knew Kendra.

He knew she hated sports.

But I was stuck with the story now.

"I know," I rushed on.

"It's kind of like teaching
a fence post to skateboard, huh?
But she asked me, so I have to."

"Oh," Ronny said. He was still quiet.

"So I'll see you tomorrow then," I said fast,
and I hung up.

Then someone behind me said,
"What a big fat lie!"

Oh, crud. Kendra.

My sister came to the door of my room.

"Lie, if you want to," she said.

"Just don't include *me* in your stories."

"Ronny asked me to go to a dance
at school," I explained.

"I didn't want to hurt his feelings."

"A lie is a lie," Kendra said.

It must be nice to be so perfect.

What did she want me to say to Ronny?

The truth?

I'd rather dance with a wet noodle.

But I couldn't *tell* him that!

"It was just a little fib," I said.

But Kendra shook her head.

"You lie a lot, Nikki!"

"Do not," I said.

"Yes, you do," Kendra said.

"What about the time you told Mom
that robbers came in the house
and ate all those brownies?"

"I was only six!" I said.

"Uh-huh," Kendra said.

"Okay, what about the note
to Mom from the principal?
You said you lost it.
And that was just last month."

Okay, so I fibbed sometimes.

But I didn't lie that much. Did I?

"Dinner!" Mom yelled.

We ignored her.

"I bet you can't go for three days without lying," Kendra said.

"Can too," I told her.

"Prove it," she said.

Kendra pointed her finger at me.

I hate that.

My sister said, "If I win the bet,

you owe me five dollars.

And I *will* win the bet."

Kendra likes nice clothes.

She's always saving up for something.

"What if I win?" I asked.

Kendra said, "What do you want?"

I thought about it.

I didn't need money.

But I was mad about being called a liar.

And I wanted Mom to believe me

about the clock.

"Okay," I said. "I'll make the bet.
But if I win, you have to say
you broke Grandpa's clock."
"What?" Kendra looked shocked.
But I didn't break the clock,
so Kendra must have.
She should just admit it.
I was tired of everybody thinking
she was Miss Perfect.
"Take it or leave it," I said.
Kendra frowned.
"You'll never win anyhow," she said.
So we made the bet.

Chapter 5
Telling the Truth

Mom woke me up at seven on Friday.

"Hey," I said. "You are all dressed up."

"I'm going to a job fair," she said.

"A lot of employers will be there.
I need to look good."

She turned around and looked in the mirror.
Then she asked it.

That question.

"Nikki," she said. "Does this skirt
make me look fat?"

I said, "Mom, you look gr. . . ."

Then I saw Kendra watching from the hall,

and I remembered.

I could not tell a lie.

I groaned.

Why do moms ask these questions?

Maybe she really wanted to know.

So I gulped and closed my eyes.

I told the truth.

"Your belly does kind of stick out."

My mom looked

like I had slapped her.

"It's not that bad!" I cried.

"It looks like a nice, soft round pillow!"

She left my room without a word.

I went downstairs, got breakfast,

and thought about things.

I was sure Ronny would get

the necklace out of the toilet.

But first I just needed to get through

a day at school without telling a lie.

Easy.

At least, that's what I thought.

I was wrong.

It was book project day.

I hate book projects, and it shows.

This time, I made a comic strip

about a chapter in the book I read.

Ms. Tims held out the paper with two fingers.

She looked like she was holding

a dead fish.

She looked like she was *smelling*

a dead fish, too.

"Nicole Riggs," Ms. Tims said.

"How much time did you spend

on this book project, exactly?"

I started to shrug.

But Kendra and I are in the same class.

I heard my sister clear her throat.

Real loud.

Oh, boy.

If I wanted to win that bet,

I had to tell the truth.

I said, "About ten minutes?"

and all the kids laughed.

Why do people think the truth

is so great, anyhow?

I don't know.

But I had lots of time to think about it

while I was staying after school

doing a new book project.

As soon as I got home after school,
Kendra said, "Nikki, tell Mom
about your book project."
"You jerk!" I cried.
I got sent to my room
for calling my sister a bad name,
and when Ronny came over,
Mom sent him back home.
The lion necklace still sat in toilet water.

Chapter 6
Home Alone

On Saturday morning,

all I could think about was the necklace.

Grams was coming back that afternoon.

I just had to get it out of the toilet

before she got home.

Saturday is chore day at our house.

I was making my bed when I saw Mom

going into my grandmother's room.

I froze.

Oh, no!

What if Mom cleaned the toilet
and flushed it?

I ran so fast to stop her that I tripped
and fell over the vacuum cleaner.

"Don't go in there!" I yelled.

"Why not?" Mom asked.

I thought then about how hard it is
to tell the truth.

"I want to clean that room today," I said.
I didn't say why.

If you only tell part of the truth,
is that the same as a lie?

Mom looked at me hard.

"It won't make up for breaking the clock,
if that's what you are thinking," she said.

"It's not about the clock!" I said.

At least *that* was the truth.

So, lucky me.

I got to clean two rooms, not just my own.

But then I did get a break.

"I'm going to the walk-in haircut place,"
Mom said.

"Who wants to come?"

"Me!" Kendra yelled.

And suddenly I was home alone.

I ran to the phone and called Ronny.

"I'm raking leaves," he said.

"I'll be there in half an hour."

Chapter 7
Toilet Trouble

I thought Ronny would bring special tools.

He brought pink rubber gloves.

"I read that soon toilets will have seats

that go up and down on their own," he said.

"They will squirt water to wash your butt.

Then they will turn the poo into. . . ."

"I don't want to know!" I cried.

"Just use the gloves!"

Ronny pulled on a glove

and stuck his hand down into the toilet water.

You could only see one corner

of the necklace down in there.

The gloves were thick but not long.

Just as Ron's fingers touched the lion,

water poured into the top of the glove.

Ronny yelled "ARRRRRGGuck!"

He jerked his hand out

and ripped off the glove.

Toilet water sprayed all over the wall.

And onto my shirt and my arm.

"ARRRRRGGuck!"

That was me yelling this time.

I looked into the toilet.

The lion had slipped farther down.

You couldn't see it anymore.

Now what?

Ronny threw the gloves in the trash

and used up every drop of the hand soap

washing his hands.

"What will happen

if we don't get the necklace out?"

I asked him.

"What if someone flushes the toilet?"

He shrugged.

"I think the necklace will just stay

in the pipes," he told me.

I was almost ready to give up.

Grams would never know what happened.

But Ronny said, "We need
something to hook the necklace.
Then we can pull it out."
I thought about what we could use.
"I know!" I said.
"What about that long fork
your dad uses for grilling?"
Ronny gave me a look.
"No way!" he said.
"We eat hot dogs off that fork!"

"We can wash it in the dishwasher,"
I told him.

"That will kill the toilet germs."

"Forget it," he said.

"Please?" I begged.

He shook his head,
but I knew he'd give in.

And he did.

"I have to rake some more," he said.

"I'll be back later."

And he went downstairs.

I ran after him.

"Ronny," I said. "Thank you.

You put your hand into toilet water to help me.

You're an awesome friend."

He turned bright red and muttered, "Okay.

Hey, maybe I'll come with you and Kendra

to the skate park today," he said.

"I always wanted to try skateboarding."

Oh. Wonderful.

My lie was coming back to haunt me.

I watched Ronny walk across to his yard.

He tripped on a stick.

I didn't know which would be worse—

Ronny dancing or Ronny skateboarding.

He turned and yelled,

"I'll be back in a little while."

But he didn't make it back in time.

Chapter 8
Liar, Liar, Pants on Fire

At noon, the door slammed.

Feet pounded up the stairs.

Mom and Kendra were home.

My sister burst into my room.

"I got my hair cut!" she said with a big smile.

She looked so happy.

"What do you think?" she asked.

Her hair was short.

It stood up in little spikes all over her head.

I did something stupid then.

I thought, "She asked for it,"

and I told the truth.

I said, "Ugh, Kendra.

You look like a wet baby porcupine."

Then I watched her smile die and

her eyes fill up with tears.

She turned and ran from the room.

I yelled after her,

"You're the one who told me not to lie!"

This thing about lying or telling the truth
is so confusing.

I guess Kendra was right.

I do lie.

I lied to Ronny.

I wanted to lie about Mom's skirt
and my book project, too.

But sometimes telling the truth
is just as bad as lying.

Worse, if you know
you're going to hurt somebody.

I thought about it for a while.

Then I made up my mind.

I was sick of always telling the truth.

I grabbed five dollars from my dresser
and went after my sister.

Kendra was facedown on her bed.

I held out the money.

"Here," I said. "I lost the bet."

Kendra didn't even look up.

"Don't you want to know how I lost?"
I asked her.

"How?" she mumbled into her pillow.

I said, "I lied to you about your hair.
It looks nice."

Another fib.

Kendra sat up then.

The top of her head looked like a scrub brush.

"Why?" she asked. "Why did you lie about it?"

I shrugged. "I don't know," I said.

"Maybe I was still mad at you about the bet."

I sat on the bed with her.

"And Mom hurt my feelings about the clock.
She blamed me, and I didn't break it."

"You didn't?" said Kendra.

She frowned.

"You really didn't?" she asked.

"Really," I said.

"But I didn't break it either," she said.

"So who did?"

Just then there was a clatter
and the door slammed downstairs.
"Helloooooooo!"
Oh, no.
Grams was back early.
I thought about the necklace
sitting in the bottom of the toilet,
and I wished that aliens would come
and suck me up into their spaceship.
They didn't.
Kendra went downstairs,
and I followed her.

Mom had the clock in her hand already.

Grams was pulling off her muddy boots.

She didn't look very upset.

"Oh, dear," she said to Mom.

"Have you been worrying about that clock

for two whole days?

I knocked it off the table myself

with that flappy fishing rod.

I was in too much of a hurry

to stop and pick it up."

She dropped onto the sofa.

"I'm sure it can be fixed," she said.

"Yes," Mom said. "I guess it can."

She was looking at me.

This time she looked sorry.

I knew she would want to talk later.

"So what's for lunch?" Grams asked.

Mom set the clock down.

"I'll get us something," she said,

starting for the kitchen.

"I'll help," Kendra offered.

"Anything but fish!" Grams yelled after them.

Chapter 9
Truth or Not?

Then Grams and I were alone.

This was it.

I felt like my mouth was filled with glue.

I had thought a lot about lying

and telling the truth over the last two days.

But it didn't help.

This was so hard.

If I told about the necklace,
Grams might get mad at me,
and Mom would be mad for sure.
But if I didn't tell, then what?
That would be like lying to Grams.
I'd be keeping a secret from her,
every day, for the rest of our lives.
I sat down beside her.
"Grams," I said. "I have to tell you
something."

"Okay, Nikki," she said, patting my cheek. "But first I have to change these pants. The cuffs are wet."

Grams went up the stairs.

I wanted to run out the front door

and keep running.

But after a minute, I got up

and walked slowly up the steps after her.

I could hear the closet door

open and close in Gram's room.

No.

Wait.

That wasn't the closet door.

It was the bathroom door.

I ran up the steps.

"Noooooo!" I yelled.

"Don't use the toilet!"

When I got to Gram's room, I heard another sound.

Flushing.

I couldn't help it.

I started to cry.

Grams hurried out of the bathroom.

She sat me on the bed

and put her arms around me.

After I stopped sobbing and hiccupping,

I told her about the lion necklace.

I was so sorry!

I said it about a hundred times.

"Nikki, stop saying that," Grams said.

"I know you are sorry.

But here is something *you* don't know."

She looked me in the eyes and said,

"I don't like that lion necklace."

I said, "But. . . ."

"Have you ever seen me wear it?"

Grams asked.

I said, "No, but Grandpa. . . ."

"I love the story about the necklace,"
Grams said.

She laughed.

"I'll never forget how funny
your Grandpa looked falling in a heap
in that car."

Then she shook her head hard.

"But I don't care about the necklace.
I care about *you.*"

She handed me a tissue.

"Now," she said.

"Let's forget this silly stuff.
What else happened while I was gone?"

I felt like a big rock had rolled

off my chest.

I blew my nose.

"Not much," I said.

"Kendra cut her hair."

"Oh, I saw!" Grams said. "She looks like

one of those welcome mats

with all the bristles."

"Don't tell her that!" I said.

"She'll cry."

"I wouldn't dream of it!" Grams exclaimed.

"I'll tell her she looks very punk,

very up-to-date."

While Grams changed her pants,

I thought about that.

Grams was not going to tell Kendra the
whole truth.

Maybe she had lied to me, too.

Maybe she did care about the necklace,
and she just didn't want me to feel bad.

I started to ask her, but I changed my mind.

I didn't want to know.

If she had lied to me, that was okay.

It was a very good lie.